RED
SUBURB

Poems by Greg Hewett

COFFEE HOUSE PRESS

2002

COFFEE HOUSE PRESS is an independent nonprofit literary publisher supported in part by a grant provided by the Minnesota State Arts Board, through an appropriation by the Minnesota State Legislature, and in part by a grant from the National Endowment for the Arts. Significant support was received for this project through a grant from the National Endowment for the Arts, a federal agency, and the Jerome Foundation. Support has also been provided by Athwin Foundation; the Bush Foundation; Buuck Family Foundation; Elmer L. & Eleanor J. Andersen Foundation; Honeywell Foundation; McKnight Foundation; Patrick and Aimee Butler Family Foundation; The St. Paul Companies Foundation, Inc.; the law firm of Schwegman, Lundberg, Woessner & Kluth, P.A.; Marshall Field's Project Imagine with support from the Target Foundation; Wells Fargo Foundation Minnesota; West Group; Woessner-Freeman Family Foundation; and many individual donors. To you and our many readers across the country, we send our thanks for your continuing support.

COFFEE HOUSE PRESS books are available to the trade through our primary distributor, Consortium Book Sales & Distribution, 1045 Westgate Drive, Saint Paul, MN 55114. For personal orders, catalogs, or other information, write to: Coffee House Press, 27 North Fourth Street, Suite 400, Minneapolis, MN 55401. Good books are brewing at coffeehousepress.org

LIBRARY OF CONGRESS CATALOGING-IN-PUBLICATION DATA

Hewett, Greg.
  Red suburb : poems / by Greg Hewett. — 1st ed.
    p. cm.
  ISBN 1-56689-129-9 (alk. paper)
  1. Gay men — Poetry. I. Title

PS3558.E826 R39 2002
811'.54—DC21   2001052947

My gratitude to the group of poets whose love and
words of counsel stream through this work:
in the beginning, Jim Cihlar and Bill Reichard;
in the middle, Karl Krause, Robert Peters, and Coco Toderan;
and in the end, Ted Mathys and Susan Jaret McKinstry.

· Contents ·

I. Cul-de-Sac

II. Cocktail

III. Buff

IV. Oculus

I.

CUL-DE-SAC

· The Distance to Birth ·

Sometimes I really kill myself,
for instance when I find myself

surprised over my own passing
youth like I've just uncovered

the gold face of some big-deal boy
pharaoh in the sand.

Through dust orbiting
in a particularly celestial

tunnel of sunlight I look out
on the park at a boy

as ancient as men get
and see he's unshaken

by the breaking news. He knew
he was old when I was born,

he knew men now petrified
in busts and those who died simply

unnoticed, he knows
October roses well,

how their dark perfumes
color the rising breeze

and still he plays with the dawn–
red leaves that circle him

as he progresses toward a shadow
blue and certain as the distance to birth.

· Nobody ·

It's easy being nobody
when you're born without a body.

To make sure this miracle was true
I let acetylene fever burn
my pale image on the sheet,
but they put me on ice as if to show
I was real flesh and bone,
their little ham I suppose.

Before I was even three
my muscle-bound uncles made me ape
Charles Atlas on the beach.
They took pictures to verify
a body that wasn't and laughed
as I made muscles of nothing.

Diseases wouldn't manifest in me.
While my siblings got leopard spots
with measles and chicken pox
and looked like greedy rodents with mumps,
I had no symptoms,
earning ginger ale with sympathetic pain.

Adolescence I simply refused.
If my arms and legs, my stomach,
even my appendix didn't exist,
then my penis, no matter
how boldly it grew
in my mind, remained untouchable.

When my father taught me to shave
I bled for special effect.
And when they fitted me for a suit,
in the tailor's three-paneled mirror stood
the reflection of a shirt going
about his business.

To myself I remained utterly
discrete, a mere hieroglyph standing for *man*.

· Glass Box ·

Growing up in an invisible house
I never knew I was home.

Even birds were unwelcome,
their soft bodies crashing into doors

that were windows and windows
that were seamless walls.

For all the light and airiness
I could scarcely see or breathe.

All signs of life were kept hidden
behind polished mirrored panels.

A fire floated at the center
of this edgeless space, cool as a star

and hearthless. No songs, no stories
disturbed the purity of line.

A glowing aquarium mimicked
our well-designed heaven.

I hugged this scrap of sea
with hope of disappearing

into a more familiar element.
Among languid angelfish I'd wait

to be reincarnated as a man
coming home every night

to an unmeasured kiss and the chaos of love,
to a clutter of furniture utterly baroque,

to a cabinet of talismans from the Amazon
and shelves of bibelots from Tunis and Japan,

to a place with real corners and real dust,
a place that would hold me in and let me out.

· Hymns to Nanan ·

1. 1960, Between the Devil and the Gulf of Mexico

Florida was never heaven—
that was Pennsylvania.
Waking to pull bright fruit
from trees for ambrosia,

and fish from the wide silver gulf
was somehow too simple when
hauling stones from the field for fences
and avoiding the poison

of rhubarb was all she had known.
But she went south for him,
taking me, a grandson, as keepsake,
or else the deceivingly prim

secretary would have taken everything
and left her with nothing but remorse.
Now jai'lai and casting for marlin,
playing the greyhounds and horses

she has bet her soul will keep him.
Only the devil knows
how far the sylvan hills
and her mother's Quaker god lie

from these infernal beaches,
these hideous swamps,
the mermaids in Miami,
and the life that he has mapped.

2. 1964, Loaves and Fish Fry (and Roast Beef)

She tore old loaves to bits,
her ritual duty
to remind us of suffering
through years of scarcity.

Pouring milk over bowls of crumbs
she'd talk about the War
and the Depression like we were there,
like we'd be eager

as our Puritan ancestors
for this meager supper,
for this ritual humility
that somehow did taste better

than Friday's exceptional fish
or the ceremony of Sunday's
rare roast displayed
before our innocent eyes.

3. 1967, Salvation

She never entered any church
and her feuds with ministers
were legendary.
She angered her sisters

with her simple prophecy
that she'd find salvation's door—
eventually—and the devil
would have to deal with her directly.

I alone was congregation,
choir, and presbytery
in her saltbox of worship
that held all mystery.

She preached to me her deity
while my heathen parents slept
with rhythms of Coltrane in their heads
and my brother and sister crept

through to watch cartoons.
She promised that if I stayed
I'd find heaven without them.
It was then I prayed.

4. 1968, Our Golgotha

The streets in town were all still brick,
a paltry legacy
of our Roman ways. She tore up
and down imperially

as I, her dwarf emperor,
sat hypnotized
by a whir under the wheels,
the humming of slaves.

Then I saw him right before us,
heading down the wooded slope,
a college student looking
like Jesus as I had hoped

in my picture-bible mind he would:
regulation beard,
long hair, gaunt face, sandals,
and those eyes of love I feared

would take me beyond her rule
to a new divinity.
Because I was her chosen one
or she just wanted me

saved for the service my crew cut
clearly marked me for
when my number was up,
she whispered right there in the Ford:

If you ever become like him
I promise you I'll steal
into your room in the dead of night
and moon or no I'll slit

your lovely white throat like a lamb,
and when you meet your God
you will not have to forgive me
for I know what I do.

5. 1969, The Flood

Don't monkey around with the moon
was her firm opinion
of all the Apollo missions.
And just as soon

as those godless astronauts stepped
onto the silver sand
the river began rising fast
and it was out of our hands.

First the glass factory went.
That furnace big as hell
where her brothers had all slaved
was doused like a coal in a pail.

Then the water swallowed each street
she'd walked for butter and eggs, for love and grief,
and when there was no higher ground
she felt righteous, relieved.

The valley where she'd spent her life
vanished at the thousand-year mark
and after praying she surmised
this time there would be no ark.

6. 1978, The Last Word

Knowing she used the word *gay*
in the old-fashioned way
I told her I was *homosexual,*
something clinical.

I didn't understand the word
had entered the lexicon
after she was born,
too late to enter

her backwoods vernacular
and I was too modern to relate
to her biblical Sodomite,
so beside her gray bed I sat

looking into blind eyes,
touching her damp forehead,
serving a silence
too strong for last words.

· When I Was Twelve ·

all I wanted
was the boy next door
home from college
to seal my chatter-
box with his
stoic Mount
Rushmore mouth
I never would have
opened
for anyone
but him
I wanted
to kiss

all day long
All day long

I chased him
round and round
the public
pool
grazing his red
nylon suit
when lucky and when
he tired
he'd throw me
far away
and up
in the sun-
blasted air

· Under the Sun ·

Through the drone of mowers,
between the cries of girls jumping rope,
under the rumble of his own skateboard

the boy detects a whispering in the grass,
and in the bed of tulips he hears
a roaring like fire underground.

Yet a still deeper silence pulls him
in widening parabolas
through the blue oak shade,

makes him believe he can escape
to the ocean floor, to outer space.

· Home From 'Nam ·

In the time before the choppy light of helicopters landing in tiger grass frag-
    mented us in our living rooms nightly,
he soared by on a skateboard looking like a trophy; soared by oblivious to tag
    along neighbor-punks like me.
He had the perfect hook shot, the meanest kick of the can, and he swam across
    seven lakes in a single summer.
He mowed the narrow lawns of our narrow neighborhood at a run, muscled back
    glistening so manly with a chevron of acne between his wings.
He smiled crooked wisecracking each afternoon with his buddies on the corner,
    he sat out late smoking on the front stoop, staring off into the radioactive
    horizon, as I wondered from my bedroom how far he was dreaming.

After, he lies beyond the lilac hedge, in a chaise longue, afghan on his lap, in ultra-
    violet May light, talking out loud to no one, because as the men in town
    put it, he had his butt blown off and wasn't quite right.
Lifting his dark glasses, blue eyes flashing, he told me to go away, that he'd been
    damned in the field when the sky had shattered like a windshield,
that there was no salvation, not in the hospitals, not even at home, where all the
    lilac suckers in the slatey earth could not choke the jungle out.

He started talking crazy about God, he cursed and cried out, he fell into the uncut
    grass and called me by name.
From under his flannel shirt brown oozed out with a stench bad as a woodchuck
    dead under the porch a week, and he begged me to help, his bag had burst,
    but all I wanted was to run.
Only when he gripped my leg did I kneel down.
Only when I wiped the cave of his belly bisected by fine copper floss did I learn love.
Only when I fit a clear, clean bag over the tube that entered into him did I know
    how much and how little there was to love.

And then his eyes turned up inside his head, lilacs started bucking in the sunny
    breeze, and I was afraid.

· Modern Living ·

It was all so modern then
when everything was so

modern. Low-slung homes
arranged in neighborhoods of

cul-de-sacs, endless front
lawns, shrubs cut like onyx.

With the whoosh of sliding
glass we came pouring out

from family rooms big as ships
to shoot up high

into the stratosphere
bright balsa-wood rockets

we hoped would land
in a blue-eye

swimming pool with
a triumphant splash.

Now these patios and pools are pitted
and cracked. Hunks of concrete

lie in yards of crabgrass.
The perfect yews have winter burn,

have taken on gothic shapes.
They tower above the split-

levels like shadows with lives
of their own. They threaten

picture windows as if
everyone has simply grown tired

of the perfect view.

· Red Suburb ·

All the watered lawns turned red,

swimming pools and miles
of blacktop and asphalt

roofs red too.
The sky is red
        not only
        as the sun
            comes and goes
            but all day and all night, even
            stars are red.

And you see things

like the red scent of lilac
or a red breeze
        moving a red swan over the small red lake,
        glittering arcs
        of golf clubs on red fairways,

a red wedding gown floating
out of church in a flood
of red organ hymns,

red envelopes shoved
through the red slot

with a clang, red piano
notes lurching uncertain
        through the air,
        red oak roots netting red cellars,

forsythia bursting red,
love moaning
                        red out open windows, red

laughter,
red stains
            on damask sheets,

a red school bus grinding
round the cul-de-sac,

red flies swarming
devil's food cake,

red milk seeping
from the sleeping
baby's mouth,
                a man shouting
                above red radio blare,

red sweat studding
a gardener's back, red noise

of mowers starting
and stopping,
                red silence,
                        the peacock's
                        long red call from the zoo,

a red canopy unfurling
over a patio,
                red shade,

three boys lighting
a pipe in the musty red
restroom at the interstate,

                    a band of girls waving red hands
                    from a dark arcade in the mall,

a couple knotted under red
                         willows at the parking-lot's edge,

a nurse arriving home
veiled in red
                 cigarette smoke,
                 sirens,
                 red crickets warring

in the grass, red tears
in a man's eyes
as he walks to his car,
                         red TV

screens lighting picture
                         windows, red whiskey
                         in a wineglass, a couple slow
                         dancing on a sea of red

linoleum,
a lone red shadow
behind that louvered window there.

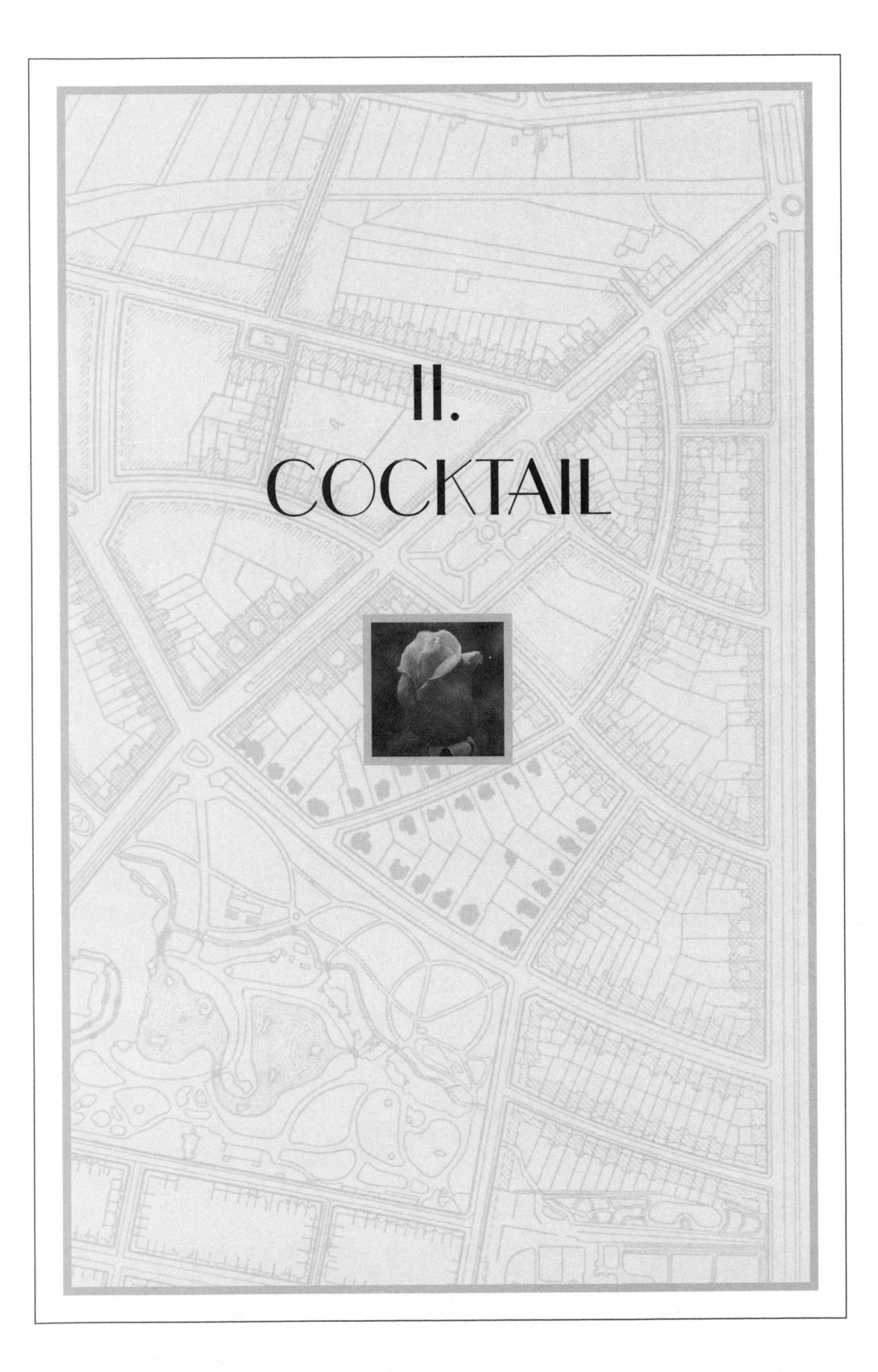

II.
COCKTAIL

· The Color of Love ·

It's clear
until I enter

an orchard of ecstatic pinks that defy
every word—*cerise, fuchsia, coral*—
and a thousand more whites than *eggshell* and *pearl*

or at night drive through all
the crazed neon in the canyon
bouncing off rain-slick pavement.

Sometimes in the poor light
of a cocktail lounge I'm sure
scarlet's the one.
Scarlet, hard-boiled,
seductive. A quiet booth,
shiny dress, shiny lips.
Scarlet for just one night.

Tramping along plateaus in the Black Hills
in September, sepia leaves me weak
for days and I forget the whole world
cannot be washed in nostalgia forever.

When I swim out into the ocean
at night, indigo goes with me.
Indigo, the truest dye.
Indigo, the depth of the universe.
Whole galaxies exist only to show indigo off.
Indigo's eternity,
indigo's oblivion

though waking on the beach
the sky turning rose
folds me in its promise.

• A Great Rose Window •

I find love by a river forgotten
as it passes through the city,
passes by glass towers and flour mills,
passes under freeways and railway trestles.
I find love and he takes me to a sumac thicket
where he shapes words inside of me to ribbons of lead,
where he illuminates words as they float from my mouth,
where every day we speak leaves of scarlet and green,
where every day we speak blue and yellow light,
where every day we breathe into the cloudless sky
above the river
a great rose window,
a great rose window
in which all the figures have been forgotten.

· The Razor's Grace ·

(spring blizzard, Grindelwald, Switzerland)

Like a prophet bellowing,
white beard a storm,
winter blew out the ascent.
We couldn't climb
the rugged face, breathe
the charged atmosphere ringing the peaks,
couldn't sound our song down oceanic valleys.
But kneeling in water I take your face
in my hands, you take mine
in yours, and as if in a mirror
we shave each other out of desire
for something sublime
as the Alps, something we have
only the echo of a word for.
Revelation comes with the fall
of whiskers, stroke by stroke
in dollops of scum.
The blood drawn
at your chin, at my throat,
streams down our lucent torsos.
We crouch in the pitted marble tub,
run clear water over our heads,
wash away any trace
of cream or hair or blood.
We stand and stare out
the darkening window where
our reflections will soon be white.

· Snowbound ·

We forget how white,
how complete,
how no words hold

parabolas
and arabesques
of drifting snow,

how everything grows
dumb in the absolute
music of this chaos.

Hear the polar
night yawning far
beyond our loneliness,

starlight falling like pins
on the tops
of the Appalachians.

See the dog breaking
boundaries, how
he flips then tunnels

not knowing the road now
blown away
and we don't call

but follow
blind to all
that's apparent:

signs and fences,
hedges and trees,
silent ghosts.

Even our tracks
in thigh-deep snow
are easily erased

and the angels
we press deep
as graves disappear.

Slowly we forget
our own bodies
and become more

or less
the undulating
landscape composed

of minute white
geometric flowers
more discrete than words.

The branches of our
lungs begin to freeze.
The silvered trees

hold fire.
We gather wood
and inside

before a blaze
our cold limbs grow
warm together.

White noise
of fire flurries
around

in our heads;
the only
articulation

the scraping
of plows still
days away.

· Prince of Light ·

Leggy and completely stripped
of its Christmas position

of honor on the credenza,
last year's poinsettia leans

toward the icy kitchen pane.
It exerts whatever will

or memory plants possess
to return to the sun-

baked terrace buried
under snow and remains

unaware it is almost
another Advent.

Maybe deep in its xylem
it is grateful to you.

I would have tossed it
with the last Epiphany.

Though the red stars are drained,
without even a trace of pink,

and the stems all woody,
fit for switches,

you remind me how
last summer it flourished

like a native, bright green
leaves dappling the brickwork.

You of course dream
a miraculous sea of red,

a whole Mexico
of poinsettias big

as trees as you trim
your patented Prince of Light

and carry it to the cellar.
You time so carefully

its daily exposure
to ultraviolet,

measure each nutrient
to the centiliter,

ready it for more
than a supporting role

beside the glass Santa Claus
and papier-mâché crèche.

All the while I tell you
for god's sake don't waste

your precious time, they're cheap,
I'll buy another,

knowing full well you'll proceed
with your labor regardless.

How I love a man who saves not
for the economy

of our modest household—
two dogs and two men—

but because the poinsettia stands
for something beyond

our means and the season,
something I have not yet tended.

· No Sign of Squirrel ·

One spring day in the blue spruce still
covered with snow, a white squirrel

                  appeared
                  like nothing

we'd ever seen.
        The little ghost just hunched there
        nearly invisible and absolutely

                    white,

not cream like lambs and no gray
undercoat like white horses,
not all yellowed either
like polar bears,
more like the snow
they hunt over, though
not quite so
blue and yet no albino,
eyes black not freakish
red like lab rats.

No, this squirrel shone

          white as milk-teeth,
          some stars,
          certain roses,
          heroin, or
          the occasional Persian cat.

Must be a sign,
        who ever heard of a squirrel white
        down to the whiskers,

a sign

though not
so obvious as the blue
peacock out the picture window
spreading his tail on the cool lawn
the day we moved in,

> that our Iranian friends said with flutes
> of champagne in their hands
> was a traditional symbol
> of good fortune and grace.

And though this is no place for peacocks

> I wanted to believe our luck
> and refused to hear you say
> he was an escapee from the zoo.

Maybe a sign
> of discontent, for the squirrel
> that occupied the spruce that screens
> our bedroom from the street
> was angry at everything,
>> at blue jays that got in its way,
>> at branches woven too close,
>> the chirping of our alarm,
>> the sun coming up,
>> angry at other squirrels getting too friendly,
>> at us making love.

That squirrel turned our bower
washed in blue-green light to hell
with its chattering high and long in stunning arabesques,
sometimes sounding like a legion
> of giant cicadae,
> at other times like a rattler lying in wait,
> or bad dope in your head.

We stopped sleeping, moved
our bedroom to the other side of the house

                    and started dreaming
                    at once white squirrels,
                    and though we cursed,
                    set traps, and put out
                    poison it ignored,

the white squirrel became our totem standing

                    for everything
                    missing.

Existence became a repeat
pattern of interlocking

           white squirrels
           and white squirrel noise,
           white squirrels quarreling
           with every quark in the universe.

And when the white squirrel vanished
with the first snow not once
raiding the bird-feeders as others do,

                we thanked God to have
                our scrap of pastoral back
                though we felt forsaken.

Come spring I looked for a sign
of the white squirrel and we returned

                to our bedroom in hope
                of coaxing him back
                but he never came
                and all disaster struck:
                I lost my job, you got sick
                of my bad luck.

A bad sign
when you said maybe that's life
                    for a white squirrel,
                    a kind of miracle

existing without camouflage,
                    easy target for raptor or cat,
                    subject to accidents like any other
                    squirrel or creature of this world.

A definite sign
           when without the white squirrel
           you walked out
           and I began to drink
           to the squirrel spirit, determining
                              that like all sacred things
                              it had been driven beyond
                              by our blasphemous ways.

Love Surrenders to Chaka Khan, or Yuki No Yoru (Snowy Night)

When you take a new lover
I'll come incognito

to your favorite
nightclub in Kyoto.

I'll send over exotic blue
cocktails and watch you

dance in submarine light
to your new goddess

Chaka Khan shimmying
on the giant screen

in all her funk splendor
taking you

to the limit, to the wire,
to the limit, through the fire . . .

I'll surrender,
I'll wander

casually out into winter
bypassing the pure

Meiji wood and paper
house we once shared

and that I once mistook
for a Shinto shrine, I'll hear

to the limit, to the limit,
to the wire, through the fire . . .

echoing off slick
black cobblestone

and you still dancing
as snow comes down

slowly covering all
the temple roofs.

· The Space between Seconds ·

I never expected forgiveness
to arrive on rainbow-tinted wings,

to speak like a fresco angel
in a streamer of gold-leaf script,

but since you closed the double-chained door
I've looked for forgiveness only

in the space between seconds
as when my eye catches a star tossed down

or a bubble rising in a moonlit pond.
I once thought I heard forgiveness in the ice

vibrating into song with the first warm wind
and once echoing hot in the empty subway.

I smelled forgiveness in a burning rice field
and swore it was emblazoned in the last red

persimmon dangling against the blue
sky smudged with smoke.

I found forgiveness for one long moment
on a winter beach, gray waves washing

over again and again the wrecked
hull of a destroyer.

· Black Creek ·

There was no TV, no jungle gym,
we played among the pines in the swamp,
played at making paradise or love.
In that sweet darkness we grew up sure and slow,
trusting ghosts and the heron's call.

One day we took up with the wind
and fell into a city with no past,
fell between church bells and sirens.
Only pigeons at the portal saw
you surrender all the years and me not call.

Give me deep shadows and your blue voice,
sing the ballad of the runaway boy
so it echoes in my head forever.
Leave your shoes, leave the future, find me lost
and we'll find the way back to our black water.

· Memorial Fountain ·

Like pale seals
boys haul themselves from the deep

marble basin where they're forbidden
and sprawl on laps of gods and heroes.

They squint in the colossal sun,
they shiver in winter's fragments,

they take shelter among columns
in a mandala of golden light

and rub blue legs together laughing
at their balls turned to walnuts.

Like soldiers they share damp smokes
and swig from the same bottle.

Over the border
of tulips rippling like a ring of fire,

beyond the plaza, in a grove
of budding oaks, the understory

overflowing with rhododendron,
in opalescent light, solitary men move

along sinuous paths, hear the archaic
laughter and remember

swimming in the fountain not caring
what lay beyond the sun-hammered paving.

· So Ecstatic, So Green ·

(on a train down the Swedish coast)

June's a green fire burning in different measure
more degrees than any December four-alarm.
Flames of pasture pour into flames of sea,
green flames rise up
above the fragile tracks.
No panic.
No outward injury.
A deeper fear that
safety glass and high speed,
thick books before our faces
and nets of words around us,
cannot protect us from a world
burning so ecstatic, so green.
Crows and gulls flutter up, ash
from a sacrifice. The final hurt,
a boy splashing through the blaze
on a red horse, in reverie.

· The Source ·

We didn't want love to end
in a rental car

on this plaza
in Andalucia

at noon. No one
crosses the shadowless

expanse of dust
except a green rooster.

At the center
a fountain starred

in the travel guide
appears far too small

for the monumental space,
the flow too weak for display,

the marble rust-stained
and slick with algae.

This trickle is all
that has come from the wild

source in a glade high
in the mountains

where that very dawn
we climbed and watched

deer the color of cream
wade into a clear green pool.

They drank so long
in the dappled light

without quivering
or glancing in our direction.

From their peace we knew
for certain we had been forsaken

and so descended
recklessly on a thread

of road, through
a labyrinth

of olive trees,
all the while eyeing

the aqueduct, hazy
at the horizon,

leaping a true line
that connects

the glittering source
to our destination

mentioned in the book
though hardly imagined.

· Märschenbrunn (Fairy Tale Fountain) ·

If I could turn love to stone
my garden would appear
like this flowerless space,
with all the frogs I ever kissed
crouched on pedestals spitting
arcs of water in perpetuity
for not making good on the prince thing.
When I gripped his soft hand
Hansel would find himself
too petrified to scatter
his bread that led me on,
glutton for his punishment
of mothers and witches.
He'd stand in the basin forever
innocent of gingerbread.
I'd see through Pinnochio
plain as the rococo
graffiti scrawled in Day-Glo
over his figure and pavement:
schwanz. I'd celebrate
gulls shattering the innocent
blue with caustic caws
and raining guano down
on this perfect artifice.
I'd wade into yew
shadows beyond, hunting for real
men who once upon a time also knew
things turned out happily
ever after again and again.

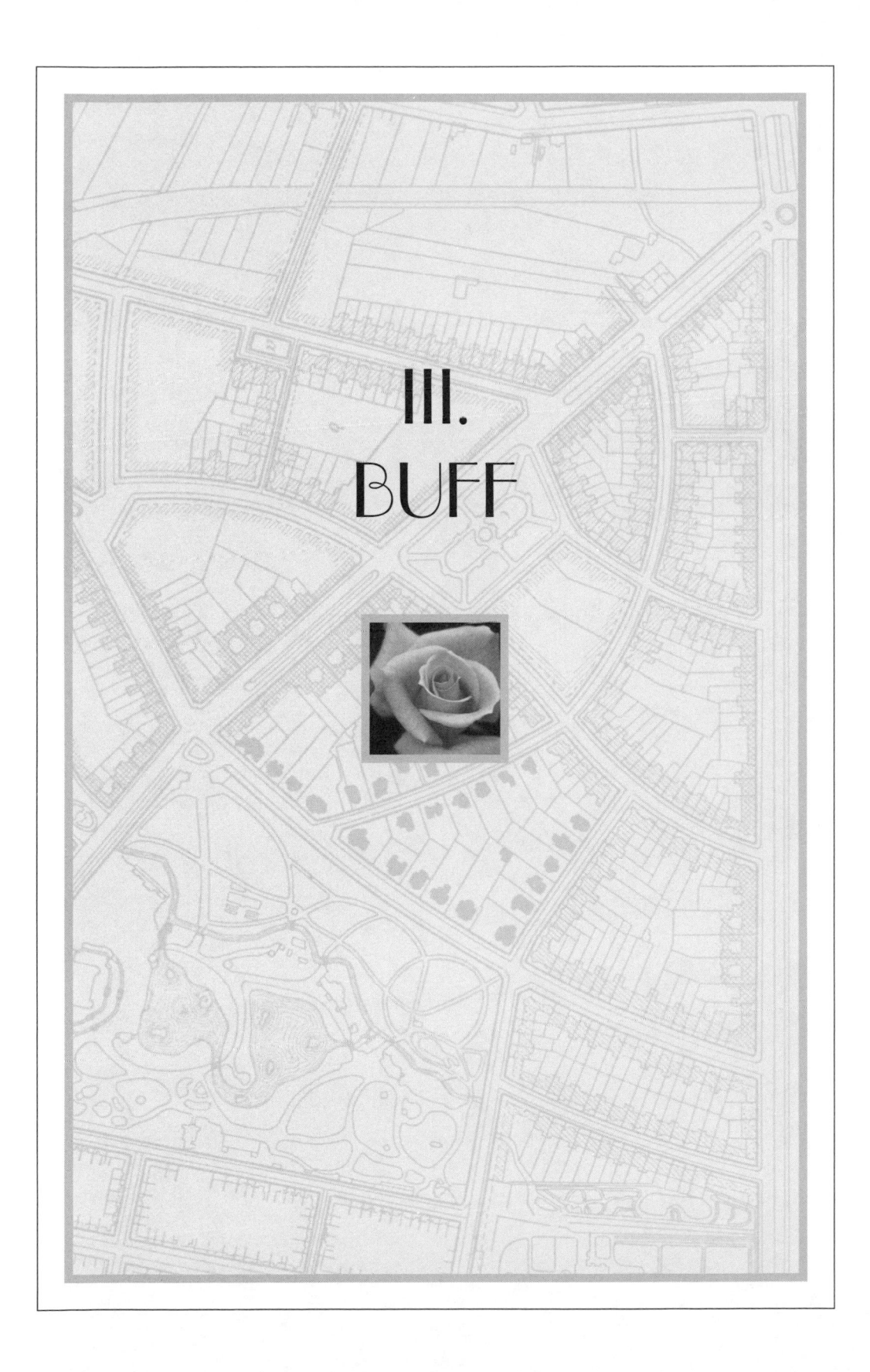

III.
BUFF

· The Next Five-or-So Years ·

Never tell the person who's going to become your lover whether you like it or not
        that he doesn't really turn you on
because he'll do crazy things right when you tell him on maybe the second date
        which is also the second time you've slept with him,
do crazy things like punch the headboard or throw the jade mountain on the
        nightstand against the wall,
and then you have to go ahead and tell him you love him anyway
because he's gotten up to stare out the window and drink a jelly jar full of
        whiskey on what's probably a moonless night or else a full moon,
which means you get up and put your arm around him and tell him you didn't
        really mean it and you want to live with him forever,
and you have sex with him right then because that's why he's so sullen,
and for the next five-or-so years all he wants is sex,
all he wants is your beauty and your body and for you to want him,
when deep down he really knows that isn't so,
so he does things you only find out in the end when he confesses,
like shredding your Speedo with a razor so no one could see you that sexy,
like taking all your letters from anyone resembling a lover past, present, or future
        and burning them on the gas grill,
like going out the whole time behind your back down to the river or over to the
        bookstore and fucking anything to feel good,
like sleeping with your friends those summers you shared a beach house so he
        could feel sexy so totally sexy,
and you're supposed to forgive him, because that's the way you are.

· I'm Not Going to Be Your Bathhouse Jesus ·

1

so don't assume too much when I give myself
to the dark room, when I put my body
in the hands of any man, not caring
for love or beauty, money or power.
Maybe you think I'm a goddamn hero
of the here and now or maybe just crazy
on crystal or just plain bored
with the not-so-few possibilities
of my cut body and choirboy smile on the street
or with my boyfriend between the sheets.

2

Thinking he's alone at the urinal,
a family man takes his wedding band off
and tucks it in his cheek like it was chaw.
I could stun him with a kiss, put his ring on
the tip of my tongue and twirl it like a song.

3

When the man with the expensive tan
acting nonchalant as a movie star
presses an amber vial of amyl
to his arched nostril and then to mine
I don't weigh his soul, I take him
deep, take every single drop
of vanity and mirror it back
simplified as lust, maybe even desire.

4

Watching the action happily
the old man beats off to the Bee Gees no longer
one iota ashamed he can't come
any closer, having learned to accept
the laws of attraction after years
of being shunned by those younger
though by no means more perfect than he.
I go to him, I grab him firmly.
He knew I'd come, he knows
every arrangement is ultimately elastic.

5

The buffest muscle punk retreats
from the dark to the showers, crowd following,
fighting like starved pups at a swollen teat.
I put my fingers to his open mouth
and he swallows them one-by-one like they were fish.

6

A boy beautiful as daylight leads me
through the labyrinth by a simple knot
at my waist, but won't kiss; I know
he only wants me on my knees for others
to watch until someone hotter comes
with good hands and a wicked mouth to match.

7

The man with an angel tattooed over his heart
begs me to love him hard, so hard,
says he's never been with a man before,
says he likes me but wishes to hell
we'd met someplace else, for instance a bar.
Sure the carpet's stained and mildew flowers
over the tile, sure the smell of semen fermenting
permeates and the pop music piped in hurts the soul,
but he meant something else, so how could I
explain that this is no better or no worse
than any other place on this sweet earth?

8

The sad man with the harelip and tortured body
holds me secure in his sinewy arms.
A scar in the shape of a dragon runs down his chest,
another, with wings, I trace the length of his back.
He smiles and the whole universe flip-flops
like a Möbius strip, and I put my mouth
to his mouth strong, and I love him most of all.

· Crimes of Lust ·

As the clubs close and I'm left
with nothing but a buzz of lust
I want you to know I'd commit crimes for you.
Though you're sleeping sober on the other side of town by now
I want you to know I'd jaywalk this empty street for you,
I'd piss a snake up and down the sidewalk for you,
drive drunk around this parking lot,
scrawl graffiti outside city hall for you.
And if it would make the morning news
I'd take a tire-iron and smash the jeweler's empty window
for you. I'd wear handcuffs,
duck into a squad car,
look right into the TV cameras just for you.

· Universes under Ball Caps ·

They say just one flash of gamma rays billions of light-years away gives off as
     much energy as the universe has had forever,
which makes sense because for example when this hot guy at the mall takes his
     cap off, his hair the color of root beer falling over his pale face can launch a
     thousand rockets flashing so fast time collapses
and I go backwards and forwards and live all my lusts at once,
from when I hung around with Lucy's Australopithecus son on the Serengeti to
     whatever alien liaison Mr. Spock could dream up.

Like Bruce Banner belted by gamma rays *boom!* I become the Incredible Hulk, all
     buff and oozing testosterone, moving through love like a cyclone,
until that guy at the mall flips those bangs back up, tucks every lock away under
     the Yankees logo, and I implode into my pedestrian form and mope on
     through the mundane,
at last understanding not only quantum physics and relativity but the mullahs
     when they deem the chador necessary
because sparks flying up from a woman's hair ignite men like stars.

· Making Tapenade ·

Pitting olives is tedious work,
it really is unless you think

of Italian boys at the beach,
their testicles ripe.

They scratch their crotches
perfectly nonchalant

as chaotic trees spring forth.
A sacred band in a sacred grove.

These unshaven boys adorned
with wreaths of seaweed,

bodies oiled and taut,
laugh easy as the wind

lifts sand up the chalk cliffs.
Sea light turns their eyes metallic.

One glances over
his salt-stained shoulder

and you feel the blade turning
toward the pit of existence.

· Cohort 1161 ·

Heat warps the sky and trees and street. The brick building melts like wax. He answers the door without a word. We both know why I have come. The room smells heavy with cat. Votive candles the only light. The one tobacco-browned window is shut. No air conditioner, no fan. I ask if I can open the window, and he says no. My skin feels like it is plastered thick with body makeup. I tell him I am a little thirsty and he hands me a smudged Flintstones glass of water, no ice. I don't rest my clipboard on the red metal table coated with grease. I am afraid these details betray us both. I write only, *Unhygienic surroundings*. The little fingernail on his left hand is long, lacquered red, chipped. His hair dirty, nylon shirt stained. Under "Personal Hygiene" I write *poor*. My eyes grow used to the dim space. I can see posters and photographs paper the walls, all of Olivia Newton-John in various poses and outfits and moods. In one she is a sailor. On empty milk crates, offerings to her: Oreos, a harmonica, plastic daisies, a bowl of clear red liquid, pieces of paper with scratched-out words on them. His face remains anonymous as an icon. His eyes follow mine. When I look at him he turns away. I do not write, *The room has become his soul*. I start the battery of questions. *Have you ever used any IV drugs? No. Have you ever used any illegal drugs? No. How many sex partners in the past week? Zero. The past month? Zero. The past year? Zero. In your life? Zero.* He has not so much as kissed another human being. I ask why he is being tested and he says, "Because I'm scared." I ask if he knows someone with AIDS, and he tells me, "No, I don't know anyone at all." I ask why he is so afraid, and he looks away. He looks at the poster from *Grease*. I ask if he wants me to leave and he says, "I called you." I ask if he is sure he wants his blood drawn and he says, "Yes." I wrap the tourniquet around his thick arm. He looks into my eyes and tells me, "I want you to stay forever."

· Ashes ·

The ashes that we scattered
off the rose-covered point

of Martha's Vineyard
and from the Golden Gate

came snowing down from heaven,
came floating down like seed.

Then came Peter and Robby
smiling like coverboys

and Victor and Kevin
buff and lesion-free

and sweet Eduardo
telling me to chill,

We're all back together,
you have nothing to fear.

Then we started dancing—
everyone I knew—

Juan, Jason and William,
Nick, Nigel and Glen—

we danced through the streets
and we danced through the park,

we danced down to the docks
and through the amber night.

But when the sun began to rise
my friends all disappeared

like shadows and fog,
like migrating birds,

and I fell back
to a world the color of ash.

· A Place More Perfect ·

So, did the hectic branches of lightning
across the plains of your wrists
guide you through the night? Are you safer now
that no quilt, no lover, no prayer will cover you,
no roof, no oak, no stars will shelter you,
happier no hand, no crow, no rain will wake you,
stronger no sign, no song, no message will tell us
Yes, I've come to a place more perfect?

· Rose Time ·

My agony came lacking thorns
and roses pulse against a sky
                    that refuses to darken
                    this noon for you.

Roses run riot,
            the island becomes a Victorian idea
            of heaven. Sweet fumes

            asphyxiate, cause tears
            to taste like candy.

Church bells echo rose,
coloring the air like a lens
                        too optimistic to correct
                        my grief-warped eye,

a rose the size of a circus tent
pinwheels through

violating my private Via
                    Dolorosa, a galaxy of roses
                    falls in the weedy lot next door,

an armada of roses tough
as armadillos overflows the harbor.

A rose like a Vegas sign announces

TODAY

ROSES CONSOLE

ALL OF BABYLON.

                                        My baby,
your roses smother my sorrow
like so many bad sympathy cards
                        though it almost really hurts
                        when the moon rises and in it I see
                        a single white rose,
                        your lost face.

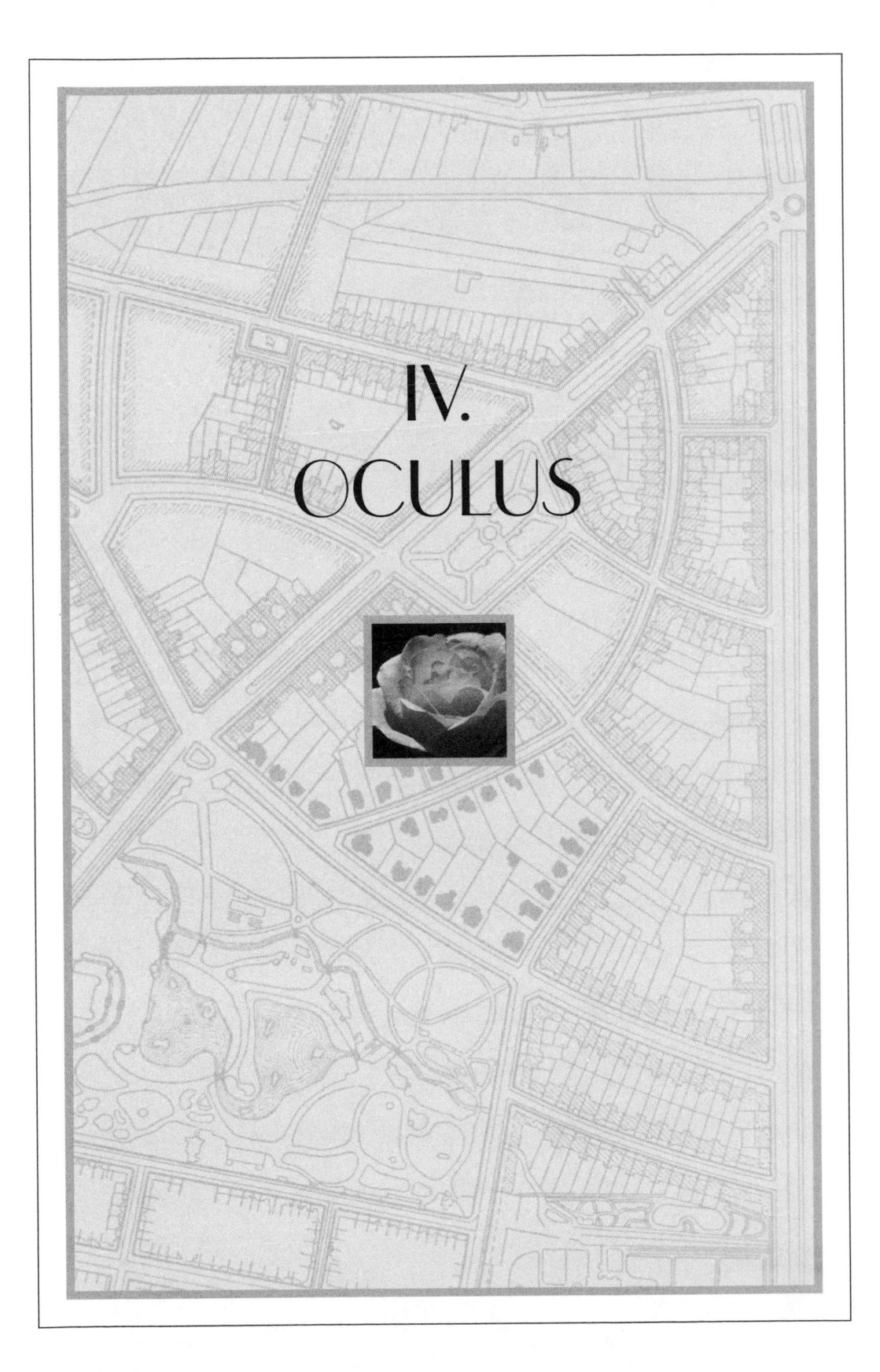

IV.
OCULUS

· Turtle Music ·

I dream my grandmother phosphorescent,
braids and arms white with fire; ragged star,
she floats through shale chambers
in the river deep underground.

I hear my grandmother's dark chant echo
in sunlight, in open air, echo
off the high walls of the gorge, echo
with the endless songs of woven water.

I see my grandmother rise under the falls,
rise and circle with the turtle
whose shell vibrates with music
of deep water and deep stone.

I watch my grandmother's flint eyes
behind the shifting screen of water
and am afraid because I keep no spirit,
afraid because through my rock-n-roll youth

I never kept the promise
to learn her song, the turtle song,
and now I cannot even hear the wind,
and now I hear secrets I do not understand

in the wind on the cliffs and under the ground.

· Bird Boy ·

I can't help it,
I see through people.

I see through the rainbow
of viscera and muscle,
past the ladder of bone,
to paths bursting like
fireworks along the spine,
transmitting information
more intricate and discrete than
binomial codes through silicon.

I see those throbbing lights
that follow all bodies,
that tell all we cannot tell.

I see through people
in the fluorescence
of the supermarket,
on the darkened street,
I see through them as I fly
over the dawn-wet park
and subdivisions alive
with television and mirage.

Some people tell me that to have
a bird's eye and wings is a gift.
I call it a curse.

I saw past my mother's Revlon mouth
down into her blue heart
and she sent me away

from her enclave in the suburbs
to the endless desert
of air-conditioned malls.

I saw through my lover's armor
of muscle to his ego thin
as mica, to his soul wasted
as a salt-stained parking lot and he left,
rusty shadow in tow.

I see through you and you see me
a condescending angel
collecting souls like trophies
in some infernal bowling tournament.

How can I explain that
I have no control
and the worst is seeing clear
through myself, a vivisected crow?

I see beneath my aura,
turned the color of sewage
from sarcasm and envy,
a mountain lake at dawn,
only my face can't seem to reflect
on the violet surface
of the indigo depths.

I see through my deep
deception of lovers
I wear like a Liberace mink,
a man naked and honest
as Orion in winter,
only he remains virtually
unknowable, distant.

I see past my drained eyes
an estuary silver with fish
and you and I sailing over,
and you and I diving down,
only it isn't clear
if there's a sandbar
on which to rest.

Though I have bird-eyes and bird-wings
I am no god, I have fallen
in love with everything I see.

· When I Lost My Hands ·

When I lost my hands I started wearing gloves,
the kind pallbearers wear,
thin and yellowed.

When I lost my hands I started to stare
at my father lifting his wineglass
like a dancer would a rose,

at my aunt shuffling cards,
brittle veins almost breaking
against the aquamarine on her knuckle,

at my grandfather holding his guitar
not so much like a lover as like a god
who has touched the earth.

When I lost my hands I started to see
how doves fold their wings
over their backs
like hands in prayer.

When I lost my hands I could no longer pray.
When I lost my hands I could no longer speak.

· Alchemy on the Charles Bridge, Prague ·

Crucifixions I know.
Erected in the middle of the stone span
our hero's twisted torso and lowered head
have meant too much to be erased by years
of soft coal burning and civic neglect.
The exorbitant flesh persists.
Back and forth I cross with desire
for any destination other than this.

Saints line the balustrades,
eyes blind from soot, tongues corroded.
Their petrified gestures to heaven
are hopelessly Baroque,
say nothing about our present need
for redemption, not even
getting old orthodoxies straight.
I can't tell if those are keys
or a quill in this one's hands,
an eagle or wheel at that one's side.
Only a nebulous mark at the base
of the Cross, rubbed by legions
of pilgrims' wishful palms,
reveals the gold finish.

I search for clearer attributes
in a stranger, one who can change
us all, who can turn a lead Jerusalem gold
in the here and now. I'm looking
for someone of a certain bent,
someone who would never convert
our history to that one crucified
Word: Love.

The skinny boy sitting on the stairs
spinning out all our ordinary agonies
on the mandolin for coins?
The girl on the esplanade drawing scenes
in oil crayon of this obscure Golgotha?

· From the 36th Floor ·

A falcon fell when I woke.
From the hotel's cornice he dropped
on folded marble wings only
to rise again. He floats
outside the pane indifferent
to Corinthian detail
and my desire.
His golden stare measures
the gilt skyline and me
simultaneously,
as last winter
he measured the Andes
and pitiful mountaineers.
He impresses himself
against the rising sun,
a newly-minted coin.
Before I can speculate,
like a balance he tilts
to catch a current that casts him
far away. I'd leap out
after my vision
if the window opened
and if I was dreaming.

· Two Sons of the King of Delhi Hanged, 1857 ·

In the shiny new museum shaped like a sun temple or camera we file past a
     daguerreotype
Of dead princes from a dead kingdom and a dead century, unmoved

Or moved as we are by other images in the gallery, for instance
Of Lincoln's killers, a mother and her son hanged with three other men in a
     row on the deck of a ship on the Potomac,

Or the police photo of a concierge in a heap of bloody crinoline
Garroted in a narrow flat in Paris not long after the time of Poe,

As much as we are moved or unmoved by the Palestinian shot dead on the West
     Bank yesterday that we saw
On the morning news, or by ancient shepherds' wells more than one hundred
     feet deep,

Black circles on the TV screen, into which we don't know
How many Afghanis threw some hundreds of other Afghanis down alive and
     grenades after them just in case, as much as we are

Moved or unmoved by the paper at breakfast showing a girl's bloody underwear
     in black and white found in a locker in Minnesota,
Or by glossy magazine pictures of holiday crowds outside a luxury department
     store in London, bleeding, bits of glass stuck in their faces

And moved or unmoved in this new museum, I want to stay
With the two boys, the princes, the sons of the King of Delhi captured

In exacting daguerreotype, executed
More than a hundred forty years ago now for, the caption says, murdering sev-
     eral British colonialists,

And unmoved or moved
I want to know how many were murdered, I want to stay

Because the mourning or jeering crowd, if there was any crowd at all,
Is already dispersed, and the landscape has not a tree or frond, flower or even
    weed

And their thin beautiful bodies just hang there with no explanation
As to why the one boy is mostly undressed while the other wears a gauzy tunic
    and ballooning trousers,

Even though they are both turbaned and both sons
Of the King of Delhi hanged, and we aren't told about justice, about good or
    evil, just the image

Taken in a place bleak as a minimalist stage set, and moved
Or unmoved, I have to know where the British are and why only a handful of
    Indian men are left watching

And why no mother mourns two sons and only
One old man looks moved, the rest unmoved, and of course the photographer
    remains

Anonymous, standing where we stand, moved
Or unmoved, and the executioners too.

· Amtrak Sunset ·

Fearing even sunsets
are insignificant
we book a domed car that insists

                on panorama, on our
                making meaning of dust and light.

From this vantage heaven is glass being blown,
the molten excess dripping
onto leafless red-twig dogwoods along the frozen shore.

For this moment high tension
wires above and lit plastic signs beyond

                      lose focus. We eclipse

another town. The universal
bowl cools. The glass perfectly clear,
perfectly black except for flaws of stars.

Satellite dishes flood living room windows
blue as the Nile, red as the lava of Iceland
and the fingers of dogwood fade away

                    from this bright world.

Our velocity blurs a trail of cows
heading for a rhombus of light.

                In the dark we catch

a rowboat turning slowly
in the river swollen to lake,

                turning among invisible red twigs,

turning under the thundering bridge,
and in that water black and blank
as a dead TV screen

        we strain to see clearly
        all that we are forgetting.

· Unnatural Acts ·

Somewhere along the line
of highway I lost nature,
                    maybe finally coming to

an understanding
I am nature even
                    amid green

destination signs
and six lanes of asphalt
where anything wild gets cut
so far back the country seems
                         distant

as the broken Lakotah
outside Sioux Falls,
South Dakota
                    hitching a ride
                    who didn't want
                    my company just the ride

and I can't say I blame him,
I have the luxury
of talking

about the nature
of things and what I feel as I
                         drive

a Toyota for hours naturally
listening to Mozart or Led Zeppelin
just to see prairie

in a park because
that's the only place left

because every once in a while I need or think
                                    I need to watch clouds

moving into each other uninterrupted,
                              need to feel
                              the sun tan my forehead

and think the prairie needs me
to witness grasses
rise exhausted from winter
                        or antelope speed away
                        to the purple ridge
                        called Blue Mounds

where I burn wild
                sage to purify
                some vague spirit
                or conjure a genuine Indian

holy vision before retiring
to the Sunset
Motel that doesn't even face west,

to a room where I'll recount
buffalo I counted
from the bison-
viewing platform
                    as I fall

into dreams
of stampede
in which I find myself